W9-CGK-871

Across the Oregon Trail

Written by Susan Brocker
Illustrated by Robert Quimby

Between the laughing and the crying,
The living and the dying,
The singing and the sighing,
The wheels roll west.

– Trail Song

CONTENTS

Introduction	The Oregon Trail	4
Map		6
Chapter One	The Runaway Wagon	8
Chapter Two	Lightning Ride	17
Chapter Three	Lost on the Prairie	26
Chapter Four	The Buffalo Hunt	35
Chapter Five	Fort Laramie	40
Chapter Six	Hold Your Fire!	45
Chapter Seven	The River Crossing	50
Chapter Eight	Across the Desert	56
Chapter Nine	The Fall	66
Chapter Ten	Into the Mountains	71
Chapter Eleven	The Shortcut	79
Chapter Twelve	The Rock of the Bear	87
Chapter Thirteen	The Way Home	95
Chapter Fourteen	Journey's End	99

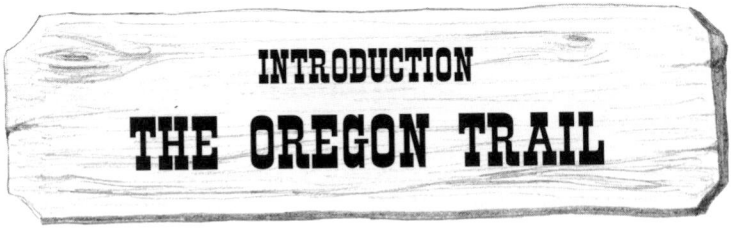

INTRODUCTION

THE OREGON TRAIL

Although this is a work of fiction, much of the detail it contains is based on fact. From the 1840s to the 1870s, up to half a million people crossed the Oregon Trail. Families packed their possessions into covered wagons, left their homes and everything they knew in Missouri, and set off overland on a long and dangerous trek to Oregon on the West Coast.

Lured by stories of a rich and beautiful land, the travelers went in search of a better life. Many of them were poor and landless and had dreams of starting up their own farms.

The 2,170-mile journey across the Oregon Trail took, on average, six months to complete. The pioneers traveled through a wild and untamed land of wide prairies, vast deserts, and steep mountains. Heading into the unknown held countless dangers. There were many deaths from disease and accidents along the way. Often, wives were forced to continue the journey without their husbands; husbands, without their wives; and children, without their parents.

Many of the pioneers who made the long journey across the Oregon Trail kept diaries of their experiences. A lot of the things that Jem experiences in this story are based upon these true accounts.

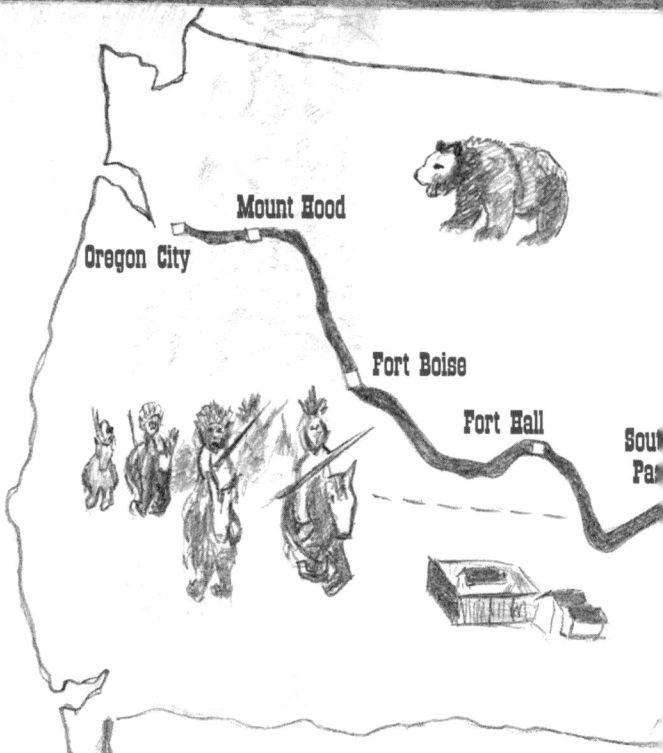

The 2,170-mile trip from Independence, Missouri, to the Pacific Northwest took, on average, six months to complete.

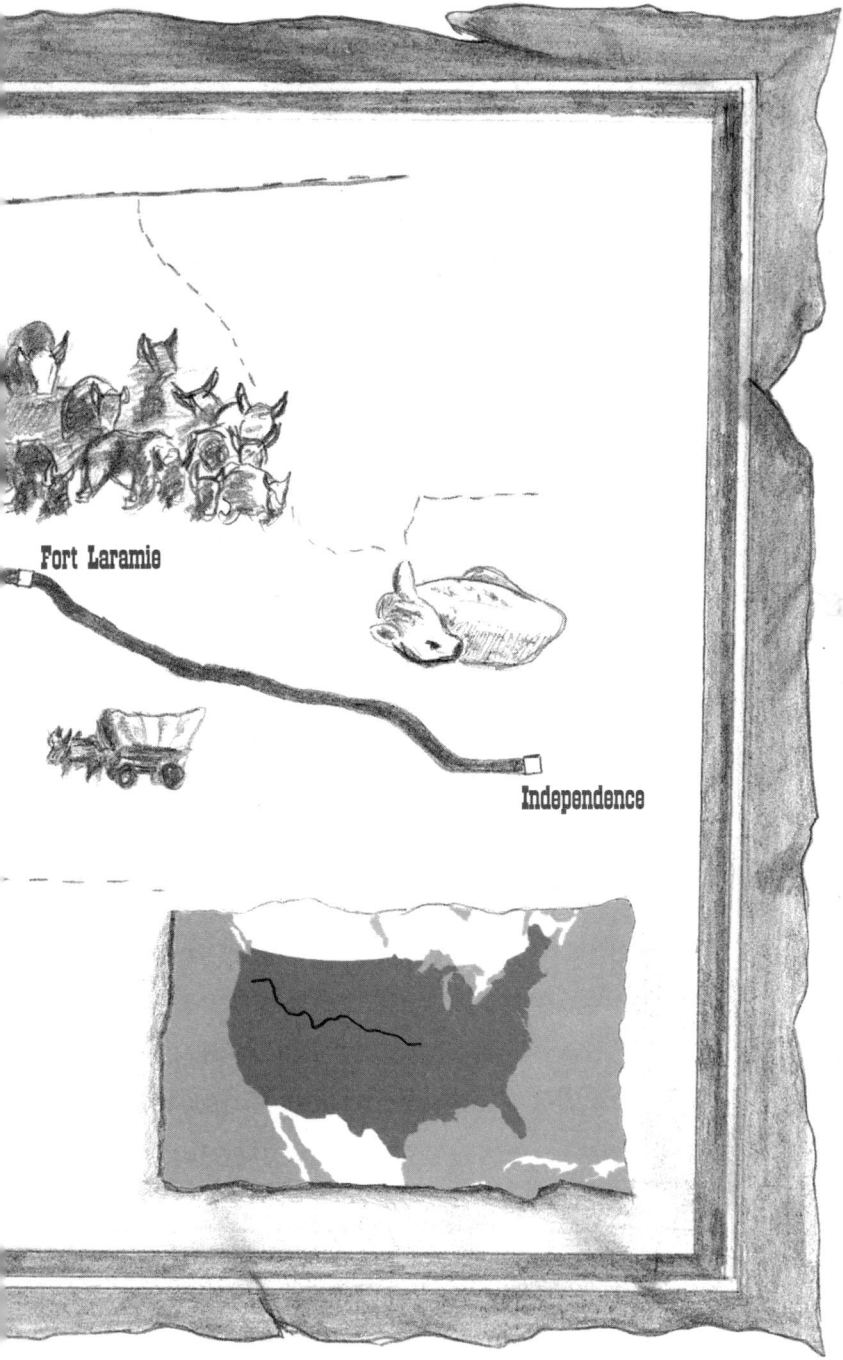
Fort Laramie
Independence

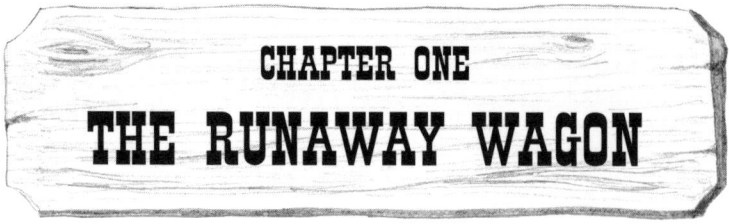

CHAPTER ONE

THE RUNAWAY WAGON

He could feel the bear's hot breath upon his face. His heart thumped so loudly he was sure it would leap out of his chest.

"Please, please leave me alone," pleaded Jem. But the grizzly kept on coming. Jem lay curled up tight, his arms wrapped around his head. The bear pushed at Jem with its snout, trying to roll him over. Jem could smell its foul breath and even see one angry red eye. Then the bear let out a roar that shattered the night. Jem screamed.

"Wake up, Jem. Wake up," called his mother. "You're having another nightmare."

Jem woke to the pitch-black darkness of the tent. His mother was gently shaking him, and his sister was muttering in her sleep, "Can't you shut him up, Ma?"

"It's time to get up anyway. The fire has to be lit and the tent packed up."

The baby started to cry in the darkness as Jem rummaged for his clothes. Outside the tent, the rest of the wagon train was stirring. Fires glimmered and dark shapes huddled in the cold. Wagons encircled the camp, their cotton canopies glowing ghostly white.

"Get up the cattle! Get up the cattle!" yelled the trail captain. He rode through the group of campers on his black mare, spurring the men into action. His rifle rested against the high pommel of his saddle, and a bullet pouch and powder horn hung by his side.

Jem hated this time of day more than any other. Out there in the dark, Goliath was waiting for him. He wondered what Goliath had planned for him today.

Along with the other oxen, Goliath was left free to graze outside the corral overnight. Guards made sure the cattle didn't stray too far, but Jem knew that Goliath would be as far away as possible.

Jem trudged out onto the plains carrying a long stock whip. The first rays of light were creeping across the prairie, and he could just make out the bulky forms of the oxen. The captain and some other men cantered past on horseback. They would round the group up and bring them all in. All, that is, except for Goliath. It was a game he played. "Catch me if you can, Jem," he seemed to say.

At last Jem saw the big ox grazing on his own behind a clump of sagebrush. He approached him from behind and prodded him with the whip. Goliath kept on munching. Jem prodded him again. Goliath still kept on munching.

"You'll never move him like that," yelled the captain from his horse. "Yaa, yaa, move on out," he bellowed at Goliath. Goliath gave him a baleful look and set off for camp at a trot. Jem had to run to keep up.

The rest of the oxen were gathered into the corral of circled wagons. Jem's sister, Ella, had already caught the team and tethered them to the wagon. "What took you so long?" she called out.

Ma was bent over the campfire cooking breakfast. The buffalo chips she'd collected for fuel were damp, and black smoke swirled about her face. Ella began to load up the wagon. It was filled with tools, spare wagon parts, small pieces of furniture, pots and pans, clothes, bedding, food for the stock, and food for the family. Everything they owned had to fit into a tiny space that measured no more than four feet wide by twelve feet long.

Jem turned to the task of yoking up the team. He approached Goliath nervously. Goliath swung his massive head around to look at Jem, his horns held high. "Look only at the eyes," Jem told himself. At least they were gentle and kind.

Jem struggled to lift the heavy wooden yokes onto the backs of the oxen. He fumbled with the collars and tangled up the traces. The oxen stamped their feet impatiently. The captain fired his rifle into the air and yelled, "Move 'em out!" The lead oxen and wagons broke off from the circle, and the rest of the train followed like a huge snake unfurling from its sleep. A line of sixty wagons soon made its bumpy way along the plains, with a straggle of men, women, children, dogs, horses, cattle, and sheep following alongside.

The prairie echoed with the sound of whips cracking, teamsters yelling to their oxen, and cattle bellowing. Teams jockeyed for position, oxen pushing and shoving and wagons bumping into each other. The captain galloped along the line, yelling commands at those who were less experienced at keeping their teams under control.

Jem could sense that Goliath and the team were restless. They were already ignoring his commands. When he called "haw" to turn left, they pulled right. When he called "gee" to turn right, they turned left. It didn't help when the captain yelled at him, "Boy, you're driving those cattle on the wrong side!"

"Greenhorn," jeered the Murphy boys, who were driving their father's team up front. "Go back to the city where you belong!"

Jem fought to keep Goliath under control. He could feel the huge beast pulling away from him. Ma and Ella were calling out to him to slow down. If only he could! The wagon was starting to grumble and groan as the wheels bounced over the rough terrain. "Whoa, whoa," he cried. The team lumbered on.

"Pull those cattle up, boy," called the captain. Jem didn't have the strength. He tried to keep alongside the team, but the massive wagon wheels rolled closer and closer until he was sure they would roll right over him. In a blind panic, he leaped to the side, and the oxen and wagon charged on ahead of him.

The oxen raced out of control. The side of the wagon smashed against the tailgate of the wagon in front, and pots and pans, food and clothes spilled onto the ground.

"Go after them, Jem!" screamed Ella. Jem could barely clamber up off the ground. The wagon slammed over a rock, teetered on one wheel, and nearly tipped. Goliath and the team galloped on, dragging the wobbling wagon behind them.

The captain rode his horse alongside Goliath and reached down for the traces. He managed to grab them, but Jem hadn't properly affixed them to the yoke. The traces came free.

"Runaways! Watch out ahead!" cried the captain. In that moment, Jem could see all his family's dreams shattered. If the wagon smashed, everything they owned would be lost and they could not go on.

Suddenly, Jem saw a spotted horse and its rider galloping up from the back of the wagon line, the boy hanging over the horse's side. They drew up alongside the oxen, and the boy spurred his horse on. Then he leaped into the air and landed on the back of Goliath. He reached over the yoke and grabbed Goliath's halter, pulling it to the right and calling out to the oxen. The great beasts began to slow, and eventually they drew to a stop, their sides heaving and froth dripping from their mouths.

"Thank you, Little Bear," called the captain. "You've saved us from a stampede." The captain cantered up to Jem, "If you can't get this team of yours under control, you and your folks are out of this train."

Little Bear stood quietly, petting the oxen. Once they were calm, he fixed the traces properly and handed the reins to Jem. Jem couldn't even bring himself to say thank you. The boy was the son of the wagon train's guide, and Jem had always been struck by how confident and sure he looked. Now, Jem felt like an idiot standing there in front of him covered in dirt.

"Had to get help from Little Bear, eh kid?" called Billie Murphy, the oldest of the Murphy boys. Ma and Ella caught up, carrying some of the items that had fallen from the wagon.

Before Jem could speak, Ma smiled and said, "The wagon's in one piece; it could have been worse."

Jem couldn't bear to look at her. He tried to turn the team back to pick up the rest of their things. Goliath wouldn't budge.

"Can't you do anything?" groaned Ella.

Little Bear gently took the reins from Jem and moved behind the oxen. "Move on," he said, clucking his tongue. They bent their backs into the traces, pulled the wagon around, then plodded on with the wagon creaking behind.

"You're standing too close to them with the whip," Little Bear said to Jem. "They see the whip from the corner of their eyes and it scares them. If you keep back and talk to them, they will understand what you want." He handed the reins back to Jem, and Jem clucked softly at the oxen. They plodded on, their ears twitching back and forth as they listened to Jem's words. Jem was in control for the first time.

Little Bear leaped up onto his spotted horse and cantered off. Jem still hadn't managed to say thank you.

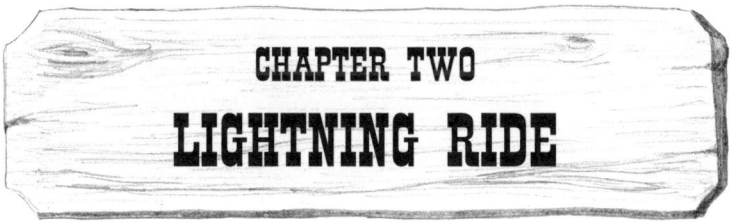

CHAPTER TWO

LIGHTNING RIDE

Since starting out on their journey from Independence, Missouri, more than a month ago, the wagon party had settled into a daily routine. They woke well before sunup, had their breakfast of coffee, bacon, and bread, loaded up the wagons, yoked the oxen, and hit the trail. There was an hour break for lunch, and at about six in the evening they set up camp. The wagons were pulled up in a circle, the tongue of each wagon butting up against the rear of the wagon ahead to form a stockade. The tents were pitched in the middle. Evenings were spent around the campfires with singing and storytelling. Jem enjoyed this time of day most of all. This was when he could escape. Nothing more was expected of him; all the animals had been tended to, the wagon checked, and any repairs made as best he could. Jem was free to read his book by the light of the campfire.

"Let's go and join the Murphys at their campfire, Jem," pestered his sister.

Ella wasn't allowed to leave the wagon alone, so she was forever badgering Jem to visit the other campfires with her. And usually it was to visit the Murphy family. Old Man Murphy was a cantankerous man, and his four sons were always giving Jem a hard time. Billie Murphy was about Jem's age, though at least a head taller. He acted like he knew it all; the trouble was that when it came to this kind of life, he really did. He'd been brought up on a farm and knew all about animals. He was always teasing Jem about being a city boy, and all the other boys joined in the teasing too.

"Forget it, Ella. Leave me alone."

"You're really boring. Why can't you be more fun!"

"Ella, that's enough," warned Ma.

At that moment, Little Bear joined them at the campfire. For once, Jem was pleased to see him. Hopefully, it would take Ella's mind off the Murphys. Little Bear and Ella had become friends since the accident with the runaway oxen. Ella was crazy about horses, and she wanted to know all about Little Bear's beautiful spotted horse. Little Bear told them that his horse was called an Appaloosa.

"Do all Appaloosas have spots like yours does?" Ella asked.

"Mostly. Some are covered all over in spots like my horse. Others have only a few spots. But all Appaloosas have eyes a lot like a human's. You can see the whites. And a lot of them have striped hooves," Little Bear said. Ella nicknamed Little Bear's horse Lightning because the stripes on his hooves looked like forks of lightning.

Jem tried not to stare at Little Bear as he sat opposite the campfire chatting to Ella. He noticed that Little Bear had a bear-claw necklace around his neck. He probably wrestled a bear to get that, Jem thought bitterly. Little Bear didn't seem afraid of anything.

"Would you like to join us for supper, Little Bear?" Ma asked. No other mother would have invited Little Bear to eat with them, Jem knew. Mostly, people in the wagon train ignored Little Bear and his father, Swift Arrow.

"I've come to ask Jem if he would like to ride with me at lunch tomorrow," said Little Bear. "He can ride Lightning, and I can ride my father's horse."

"I'm sure he'd love to," Jem's mother said before Jem had the chance to say no. Jem wished his mother hadn't answered for him. The last thing in the world he wanted to do was ride Lightning.

That night, Jem couldn't get to sleep. He dreaded the thought of riding Lightning. What if he fell off and made a fool of himself? Jem had only ever ridden their old gray mare Tess, and she never went faster than a walk. Lightning pranced and reared and tossed his head and could move as fast as his name. Jem was sure he would have nightmares about it.

When Jem eventually did fall asleep, however, it was not Lightning that he dreamed about. It was something far more frightening. The grizzly bear came back again. This time, it had Jem by the neck and was shaking him like a rag doll. Jem woke up screaming once again.

Noon the next day, the captain rode down the straggling line of wagons, calling everybody to a halt for lunch. It had been a long hot morning. Jem loosened the traces on the oxen for them to rest. It was tiring work pulling the wagons in the scorching sun. Ma and Ella were tired too. At the start of the journey they'd ridden up front on the wagon, but the ride was incredibly bumpy and uncomfortable. Now they took turns walking with baby

Matthew and riding on Tess. Their feet ached from trudging across the hard ground.

Jem hoped that Little Bear might have forgotten his offer of a ride, but as soon as the wagon party had settled down to lunch, he rode up on his father's horse, leading Lightning. Lightning was wearing a wooden saddle covered with wolf skin and decorated with beadwork. Beadwork ornaments were attached to his bridle and stirrups, and a woven breast collar hung around his neck. He looked impressive.

"I thought we could ride over to that outcrop of rocks," Little Bear said, handing Lightning's reins over to Jem. Lightning danced and snorted, and Jem's stomach turned. He managed to get his foot in the rawhide stirrup and swung up into the saddle. All the while, his stomach was doing little flips. To his surprise, sitting on Lightning's back felt great. The horse's dancing step was smooth and gentle like sitting in a boat dipping and ducking on the waves.

"Do you want to go for a canter?" Little Bear asked.

"Yes, I think so," replied Jem.

Little Bear clicked his tongue, and before Jem had a chance to wonder if he was doing the right thing, Lightning was off. Jem had never gone so fast in all his life. He leaned over the horse's neck and watched the ground disappear beneath the flashing hooves. He heard himself yipping and yelling, and then they were passing Little Bear and his horse. The two boys raced toward the outcrop of rocks. Lightning's mane was flying in Jem's face and the wind was whipping through his hair. When they reached the rocks, Jem and Lightning were well out in front.

"That wasn't a canter, that was a gallop!" laughed Little Bear as he pulled his horse to a stop.

"It was flying!" Jem grinned, patting Lightning's neck.

The boys turned their horses back to camp. The huddle of wagons up ahead looked tiny in the vastness of the plains. It seemed to Jem that you could see forever across the rolling plains, with the long golden grasses moving like a restless sea in the wind.

"Do you ever get tired of this flat land?" Jem asked Little Bear.

"Yes, I miss the mountains and the lakes. I would like to go home."

Jem was surprised. "You mean you don't live on the plains? Where are you from?"

"My family and I come from the mountains to the northwest. Far away. It's near the place you're heading. That's why my father is guiding the group. He knows the mountains very well."

Jem wanted to know more. He thought that all Native people lived on the plains. He knew Little Bear was Nez Perce, but he thought it might be rude to ask too many questions. Instead he said, "Lightning is a wonderful horse. He's very special."

"The Nez Perce have bred the spotted horse for many years. Only the fastest and cleverest horses are chosen. They run free in the valley where my people live."

Jem rode Lightning proudly into camp. The horse pranced and danced, and Jem sat still and deep in the saddle the way Little Bear had shown him. Billie and his brothers gawked as he rode by.

"City boy didn't fall off the big scary horse, then?" Billie Murphy called out.

Jem hoped that Ma and Ella would see him riding Lightning so confidently, but as they rode up to the wagon, his sister and mother were too busy fussing over a tiny fawn to even notice.

CHAPTER THREE

LOST ON THE PRAIRIE

Ella was trying to feed the tiny fawn from a mug. She was spilling more on herself than down the fawn's throat.

"Where did that come from?" Jem asked as he dismounted Lightning.

"I found her in those trees over there," Ella said, pointing to a stand of cottonwoods by the camp. "She was fast asleep, all curled up in a tight ball!"

"You should return her," said Little Bear. "Her mother has left her there for safekeeping while she goes out to graze. She'll be back for her soon."

"But she followed me back to camp. She's lonely. She wants to stay with me!"

"Perhaps you should listen to Little Bear, Ella. She'll die without her mother," Ma said.

Ella made a face and said she would return the fawn. She wandered out of camp with the little fawn wobbling behind on her stiltlike legs.

By the time they'd packed up, Ella had returned. "Move 'em out! Move 'em out!" called the captain, and the wagon train rumbled out across the plains. Jem walked behind the plodding Goliath. He no longer needed to carry a whip – they understood each other now. Most of his time could be spent daydreaming. This afternoon Jem thought a lot about riding Lightning. He wished his father could have seen him. He would have been proud.

The wagon train made slow progress in the hot sun. When they reached a swift-flowing stream, the captain decided they could stop early for the day to give the cattle a rest and to catch up on repairs. Some groups went down to the stream to wash the dusty clothing, and the children followed to splash around and cool off. Ella was the first to go, forgetting her chores and leaving it to Jem to collect buffalo chips for the fire.

While Ella, Ma, and Matthew were gone and the rest of the camp was quiet, Jem heard a plaintive bleating coming from the back of the wagon. He climbed onto the wagon tongue and peered in. There in the corner, tucked up in Ella's bedroll, was the fawn. Jem was furious. Ella never listened.

Jem took Ella aside when she returned. "Ma told you to take that fawn back to her mother. Do you know what's going to happen now? She's going to die, that's what! You can't feed her. Only her mother can do that."

"It's not my fault. I tried to return her and she followed me back. I couldn't desert her! Please don't tell Ma; she'll never trust me again."

Jem felt sorry for Ella. He also knew that Little Bear was right – the fawn would die without her mother. "I'll take her back while Ma's doing the chores. It won't take long on horseback."

Before his mother could return and ask him what he was up to, Jem saddled Tess and set off with the fawn nestled in the saddle pack. It was easy to retrace the wagon train's path as the wheels had flattened the prairie grass and left ruts in the soil. Finally he reached the area where they'd camped for lunch and found the cottonwoods. He placed the bleating fawn under a tree and rode off to a safe distance. Soon a deer approached and Jem watched happily as mother and daughter were reunited.

It wasn't until the light began to fade that Jem realized he'd been away far too long. Night fell rapidly on the plains, and shortly he would be unable to see the way. He hadn't even brought a lamp of any kind or even any matches. He was terrified of spending the night out on the prairie alone, but he'd left himself little choice.

The night was inky black. There wasn't even a slice of moon to light the way. Tess stumbled as they wandered aimlessly in the dark. They would have to stop and wait until morning to find the path. He unsaddled the mare by touch as he couldn't even see the girth or straps. Then he groped around for a heavy rock and rolled it on top of the reins to keep the horse from straying off. He lay down on the hard ground with his head against the saddle.

It was chilly after the searing heat of the day. Jem shivered and pulled the saddle blanket around his shoulders. Close by, coyotes yapped to each other, and in the distance wolves howled into the night. Jem thought of the graves he had seen along the trail – graves of travelers who would never make it to Oregon. Many of the graves had been dug up by wolves and the bones scattered across the ground. Sometimes the wolves circled their camp, though they never came close with all the people around. But one boy on his own...? Jem picked up a big rock.

He clung onto the rock through the long hours, listening to the howling of the wolves.

At some stage he drifted into a fitful sleep, the sounds of the night forming the backdrop to a horrible nightmare. In the nightmare he was trying to run. His legs wouldn't move. Something was coming up behind him, and it was coming up fast. It slammed a mighty paw upon his shoulder. The grizzly! The grizzly had him in its grip and was shaking him. Jem screamed out, "Leave me alone! Leave me alone!" He awoke to find Swift Arrow's hand upon his shoulder.

Little Bear's father pulled Jem to his feet. His horse and the old gray mare stood side by side in the pale light of dawn. Without saying a word, Swift Arrow saddled the mare and hoisted Jem onto the saddle.

They rode in silence for a long time before Jem could overcome his embarrassment and say anything.

"Thank you for coming to find me," he said to Swift Arrow.

"I didn't find you. You weren't lost. I told your mother that you would know the way and catch up with us by daylight. But she was worried."

Swift Arrow actually believed that Jem could have found his way back on his own! He wouldn't tell Swift Arrow how scared he had been.

They rode on across the prairie, Tess trying her best to keep up with the long strides of Swift Arrow's horse. The horse was an Appaloosa like Little Bear's. It had white spots like a sprinkling of snowflakes across its back.

"Little Bear says that in the valley where you live there are lots of Appaloosa horses."

"Yes, there are many. Little Bear misses the horses. He misses the valley also. Sometimes, he weeps at night for his home."

Jem was surprised. He couldn't imagine Little Bear crying. He always seemed so brave.

As they rode, Swift Arrow pointed out many things on the prairie that Jem had never noticed before. He showed Jem the rutted paths made in the earth by the buffalo herds as they moved down to drink from the wide waters of the North Platte River. He pointed out the wavering patterns that had been made in the sand by a passing rattlesnake and the little mounds of earth piled high by prairie dogs.

Eventually, the white canopies of the wagon train came into sight up ahead. Before they reached the first few stragglers, Swift Arrow turned to Jem and asked, "What is it that frightens you as you sleep?"

Jem would have shriveled up and died had anyone else asked him that question, but somehow it didn't seem so bad coming from this man.

"It's a bear. I have nightmares about a grizzly bear."

"You must make your peace with the bear," Swift Arrow said. "Look it in the eye and say, 'Bear, I am not frightened of you! Go away, and don't come back until you can be friendly.'"

Jem doubted very much that that would work. Swift Arrow had not seen his bear. He had not looked into its angry red eyes or smelled its foul breath. But he promised Swift Arrow that he would try.

CHAPTER FOUR

THE BUFFALO HUNT

Day after day, the wagon train lumbered over the plains. To the travelers, it felt as if the prairie would never cease rolling on ahead of them. The days dragged along with the dragging of their tired feet. The younger children amused themselves collecting wildflowers, playing games, and riding bareback on their ponies. The adults watched out for buffalo and other game. Fresh meat made a welcome change to an endless diet of salted bacon.

Whenever a herd of buffalo was spotted, it caused great excitement. Any man not in charge of an oxen team would grab his rifle and charge after the herd. The buffalo hunting wasn't always a great success though. Most of the men were farmers, not hunters, and they didn't have a lot of experience with guns.

In fact, there had been several accidents already. One man had even shot off his own foot. Jem wished that he had a rifle, but he doubted he'd be capable of hitting anything if he did, not even his own foot.

Sometimes, they saw large groups of Native people on the move. Their long lines of ponies trailed through the waving grasses. The ponies dragged poles lashed to their sides. Hide was stretched between the poles, and the hammocks carried tepees, skins, baskets full of cooking utensils and food, bundles of clothing, and babies in their cradles. Dogs trotted alongside, some pulling their own small carts loaded with gear. Little children ran and played among the group, and some children rode astride their shaggy ponies.

"Where do you think they're going?" Jem asked Little Bear.

"They're following the buffalo herds as they migrate."

"Do your people follow the herds too?" Jem asked Little Bear.

"Our hunters come down to the plains to hunt the buffalo, but we do not follow the herds. We live mainly in the high country, where we hunt in the woods and fish the rivers and streams."

One morning, they heard a noise that sounded like distant thunder. The noise grew louder and the oxen began to pull restlessly in their traces. On the horizon they could see a massive black shape fanning out and coming toward them. From a distance it looked as if the ground itself was moving like a black sea.

"Hold back your cattle!" yelled the captain. "Buffalo stampede!"

Jem had never seen or heard anything like it. There were so many buffalo thundering toward them that he couldn't have counted them if he'd tried. The noise was deafening. Jem was sure the black mass of buffalo would run them down. At the last moment, they swerved and thundered off in the other direction.

Men grabbed their rifles and horses. Yipping and yahooing, they galloped off after the buffalo. Jem stood watching them with a mixture of envy and fear. He imagined what it would be like to fall off a horse and be trampled by thousands of hooves.

"Come and ride with me," Little Bear called. He was riding bareback on Lightning. He grabbed Jem's hand, pulling him up behind him. "Hang on and you'll be fine," he said.

Little Bear whirled Lightning around, and they galloped off after the others. Jem clung onto Little Bear with all his might. They were soon neck and neck with the vast herd. One huge bull was running on the outside. Little Bear cut him off from the rest. The bull pounded across the plains, his short tail held high and shaggy head lowered. Little Bear dropped the reins on Lightning's neck and pulled an arrow from his quiver. He fired the arrow and hit the bull in the chest. The bull thudded to the ground.

Little Bear pulled Lightning to a stop. Jem looked ahead at the retreating buffalo and the riders whooping after them. "Quick, Little

Bear. We can still catch up," he called out excitedly.

"You can only carry so much meat in your wagon," Little Bear said. "There is no need to kill any more."

The family had fresh buffalo steaks for dinner that night. Little Bear showed Jem how to cook the buffalo meat and cut it into thin strips to dry. Before Jem went to bed, Ella whispered that he'd been brave to go hunting with Little Bear.

Jem felt good as he fell asleep. Perhaps that was why he wasn't expecting the grizzly. It sneaked up in his dreams, a huge beast the size of the buffalo Little Bear had killed. It lowered its shaggy head as if it were about to spring on Jem and sink its claws into his neck. Jem was petrified. Then he thought of Swift Arrow's words. He looked the bear in the eye and said, "I am not frightened of you. Go away!" The huge bear growled at Jem, pawed at the air, and turned and shuffled away.

CHAPTER FIVE

FORT LARAMIE

The ground was becoming sandy and strewn with rocks, and the hooves of the oxen stirred up clouds of thick dust. The wagon train split into small groups to reduce the amount of dust thrown up into the paths of the following wagons. Along the way, they passed by the strangest rocks that Jem had ever seen. Some looked like towering castles of gold. One jutted out of the ground like a gigantic finger pointing to the sky. The captain said it was called Chimney Rock.

At last, the tired and weather-beaten travelers reached Fort Laramie, a trading post and the gateway to the Rocky Mountains. They were now a third of the way to Oregon City. At Fort Laramie, they would rest for four days, carry out wagon repairs, and buy supplies before setting out on the steepening ascent to the Rockies.

The fort was built of clay bricks dried yellow in the hot sun. The buildings formed a large square guarded by a timbered gateway and two-storied blockhouses. The wagon party set up camp outside the fort, only some of them staying inside. Jem envied them sleeping in beds and sitting on chairs.

Jem was fascinated by the people he saw inside the fort. There were hunters and trappers from the mountains and Native Americans from many different tribes. The mountain men had weatherworn faces, long straggly hair, and wore fringed buckskins. They'd all come to talk and to trade. Jem overheard one trapper telling a yarn to the others, "It's so windy up there that you could walk for ten minutes and end up three feet *behind* the place you started!"

Pack mules were tied up to the railings and loaded high with buffalo and beaver skins. The fort rang with the constant hammering and banging of blacksmiths' tools. A massive bearded man with a heavy accent was helping to repair a smashed wagon wheel. Another blacksmith was shoeing oxen with sturdy iron shoes, preparing for the rocky trail ahead.

Some of the wagon party made the decision to turn back at Fort Laramie. The trip was tougher than they'd expected, and they weren't prepared to go on. Secretly, Jem hoped his mother would come to the same decision, but the night before, she'd turned to Jem and said, "I know this trip has been hard on you since your father died. But he would have wanted us to go on. We can have a much better life in Oregon. Don't you worry, Jem. We'll be just fine."

Inside, Jem was screaming, "No!" but he thought of his father and the dreams he'd had for the family. Although his father had been a skilled tradesman, he'd found it hard to get regular work in the city. He'd heard the stories about Oregon and life on the

New Frontier. Land was cheap and good for farming, and he dreamed of his family owning their own farm. He'd spent their entire savings outfitting them for the trip. "I can do it, Ma." Jem said, wondering how he was ever going to get them through the next thirteen hundred miles.

Now they would have to buy extra provisions for the journey ahead and get rid of the useless things they'd packed in the first place. The oxen were struggling to pull the heavily loaded wagon over the tougher legs of the journey, and Jem's mother decided to trade in the few items of furniture they were carrying. The Murphys told her about a trader at the fort offering to barter goods for produce.

Jem found the trader selling goods from the back of a wagon loaded with barrels, baskets, books, clothes, furniture, and even a grandfather clock.

"Sir, would you consider trading some supplies for this jewelry box? It's very old," Jem asked the trader.

"Now sonny, what would I do with a jewelry box way out here?" The trader added, "But seeing as how you're so polite, I'll give you a bag of sugar for it." Jem didn't think that sounded very good at all, but he'd heard how expensive things were at the fort and knew he had very little choice.

That evening around their campfire they all looked forward to sugar in their coffee. Ma set the pot to boil, and Ella opened the bag of sugar. Jem stirred his coffee and took a sip. It wasn't very sweet. He sipped some more and got a mouthful of grit.

"What's the matter, greenhorn? Got grit between your teeth?" called Billie Murphy. The Murphy boys collapsed into laughter.

Jem checked the bag of sugar. It had been mixed with sand. What a fool he'd been! Why had he trusted anything that the Murphys said? They loved to make him look stupid. They knew that the trader was a swindler.

When Jem went to the fort the following day, the trader and his wagon were gone.

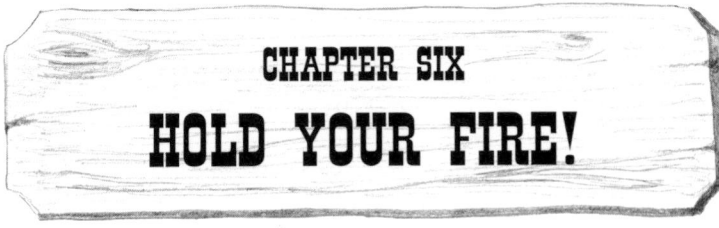

CHAPTER SIX

HOLD YOUR FIRE!

They smelled them before they saw them. The hot breeze picked up the cloying smell of the rotting carcasses and assailed the travelers. Up ahead, buzzards circled restlessly in the sky. Wolves, disturbed by the approaching wagon train, slunk off into the distance. It wasn't until the wagon train reached the river that Jem saw the mounds of buffalo carcasses spread like black pebbles over the valley floor.

The wagon train was ten days out of Fort Laramie and following the winding course of the North Platte River. Three days before, they'd been passed by a band of heavily armed men. The men were impatient to cut through without spending time to chat, unusual on the trail where meeting others was a way of passing on information and news.

The men had obviously had time to stop for some sport, however. Hundreds of buffalo lay dead and rotting. They hadn't been butchered for their meat nor had they been skinned. The only things missing were their tails.

The captain rode among the carcasses. He returned to the wagons and yelled, "This won't look good for us. The Sioux will be angry if they see this slaughter." His words sent a ripple of fear among the wagon train. Since their journey had begun, many of the travelers had feared attacks from Native people. But all along the captain had reassured the wagon party that they were friendly. He told them of times when Native people had helped pull out stuck wagons or assisted in dangerous river crossings.

Jem spoke to Little Bear about it later. "Do you think we have anything to fear from the Sioux, Little Bear?"

"The buffalo are sacred to the Native people. But the Sioux will already know who did this."

Early that afternoon they reached a massive slab of rock that looked like a gigantic turtle lying on the plains. Travelers had nicknamed it Independence Rock because wagon trains on the trail often made it to the rock in time for Independence Day. Jem and his party were a few weeks late, but they aimed to celebrate anyway. Any thought of reprisals was forgotten as the party prepared for a dance that evening. Ma was even making a special pie from berries that Ella and Jem had picked along the trail.

Ella, Jem, and Little Bear rode the horses over to the rock and scrambled up its steep side. They climbed higher and higher until they could see right across the valley down to the wagon train camped below. The rock was peppered with holes and crevices, and travelers had chiseled their names and messages into the granite. With a sharp stone, Ella chiseled her name in big letters: "ELLA WAS HERE, JULY 1847."

It was Little Bear who first saw the riders approaching from the west. There were about seventy of them riding fast and hard across the valley floor toward the camp. "Sioux!" Little Bear said. "We must warn the captain." The three scrambled down the rock as quickly as they could without stumbling headfirst. Little Bear leaped onto Lightning and pulled Ella up behind him. Jem got on Tess's back and yelled, "Go on ahead and tell the captain. I'll follow as fast as I can."

Jem reached the camp to find it in turmoil. The wagons had been drawn into a circle, and the tailgates of each were raised and locked into the one ahead to form a barrier. Men had grabbed their rifles and taken up position beneath the wagons, and the women and children were taking shelter behind the huge wheels. Jem's mother saw him ride up and screamed for him to take cover. Behind him, Jem could hear the thunder of hooves. He dived off the horse and threw himself under the nearest wagon.

The captain was yelling instructions at the top of his voice, "Hold your fire! I repeat, hold your fire!"

Jem heard a rifle shot. At first he thought it was the Sioux firing, but then he realized they weren't even carrying guns. Then he saw one of the Murphy boys kneeling on the tailgate of a wagon. He was trying to reload his rifle to fire again. Before he even got the chance a man rode up at full gallop, leaned out from his pony, and snatched the rifle straight out of his hands. The Murphy boy was left on one knee with his hands up, frozen to the spot. Jem had never seen anyone look so surprised.

The rest of the Sioux group came cantering up and exchanged greetings with the captain. They had simply come to trade.

CHAPTER SEVEN

THE RIVER CROSSING

The wagon train pushed on across the Oregon Trail, following in the footsteps of others who had gone before in search of their dreams. Many hadn't made it. All along the trail were the graves of men, women, and children. Some were marked with small wooden crosses; others had only a mound of stones to keep the wolves at bay. Jem's mother always made a point of stopping and placing wildflowers on the graves.

In one lonely spot, they came across a solitary wagon and its sad occupants. The mother and father were very ill and too weak to continue their journey. The wagon train they were traveling with had been forced to go on without them. Their baby lay dead in the wagon; they didn't have the strength to bury her. Swift Arrow dug a grave for the little girl, and they left the couple with what medicine and comforts they could. As the wagon train pulled out, they all knew the couple wouldn't make it through the night.

In the early hours of one morning, Jem and his family were awakened by a massive crash of thunder. Lightning cracked open the heavens, and rain began to drive through the canvas of their tent. In seconds, their bedding and all their belongings were soaking.

"Grab what you can and head for the wagon," Ma cried. Outside, the camp was in chaos. As the lightning struck overhead, it lit up the whole valley. Jem could see other families struggling to lash down tents and calm the frightened horses. He tied down the tent guys as best he could and ran to the shelter of the wagon. Ella and Ma had lifted out the barrels and sat huddled in a corner. Matthew was screaming as the thunder crashed above their heads.

U U U

The wagon train looked like a traveling clothesline as it pulled out the next day. Bedding and clothes hung from the wagon hoops and flapped in the warm breeze. Sodden tents lay draped across the wagon tongues, drying in the sunshine. The oxen and wagons ploughed through a trail of thick mud. The wheels got stuck up to the axles, and several wagons had to be dug out from the brown ooze.

When they reached the banks of the Sweetwater River, they found its waters swollen by the overnight downpour. "Our trail lies beyond the river. We have no choice but to cross," the captain called out to the party. Swift Arrow rode out into the river to see where the safest crossing could be made.

Jem's heart began to race as he watched Swift Arrow wade out into the water. He wanted to yell out, "Turn back!" In that instant, Jem was reminded of the day his father died. His father had been wading out into a wide river at the start of their journey when he'd suddenly gone down.

His father had struggled in the swift currents for some time. They said he'd quietly slipped beneath the waters only moments before Jem had reached him.

"Lead the teams out slowly and there should be no problems," Swift Arrow called out from the opposite bank. Jem's mother touched him gently on the arm, "Come on, Jem. It will be fine." The leading teams clambered down the riverbank and into the river. They were soon up to their chests in water that lapped at the wagons' running boards. Goliath seemed happy to follow, and the team headed down the bank. Jem led them into the water as Ella, Ma, and Matthew sat up on the front seat.

They were halfway across the river when Tess got loose from her tether at the back of the wagon and decided to swim off. Ella saw her and cried out, "Tess! Tess come back!" Without thinking, she leaped off the wagon and into the water and tried to swim after the horse. She was quickly in over her head. Ella was not a good swimmer. The current was strong out in the eddies. She began to struggle and go under.

Fear gripped Jem until it nearly paralyzed him. He hadn't been able to save his father; what if he couldn't save his sister? He dived out into the middle of the river and swam toward Ella. As he surged through the water, the same horrible thoughts went through his head. What if he failed again? What if Ella drowned before he could reach her? After what seemed like an eternity, he had ahold of her arm. He dragged her out of the strong current and to the riverbank. She lay in the mud trying to catch her breath. She was safe.

That night, Jem dreamed of the grizzly bear again. It came shuffling up to him with its awkward rolling gait. But this time, Jem did not feel frightened. Instead, he reached out his hand to the bear. It stopped before him and took his hand gently in its huge mouth. It sat up on its haunches and playfully boxed Jem with one gigantic paw. The grizzly wanted to be friends.

CHAPTER EIGHT

ACROSS THE DESERT

Since Independence Rock, the trail had gradually become an uphill climb. The wagon train grinded up steep ridges and across boulder-strewn riverbeds. The oxen struggled to pull the wagons up the rough tracks. It broke Jem's heart to see their feet cut and bleeding from the sharp stones. Goliath battled on bravely with his strength and determination, pulling the rest of the team through.

Jem and his mother agreed that they would have to try to lighten the load further if the oxen were to complete the journey. They tossed out any items that they didn't depend on for survival. Even things that they would need to set up their new home were tossed out. Others in the train were forced to do the same. The trail was littered with pieces of furniture, luggage, blankets, clothing, wagon parts, tools, plows, and slabs of dried meat.

The travelers looked forward to reaching South Pass. Here they would cross the Continental Divide and pass into Oregon Country. They expected the pass to be dramatic, a narrow path through the Rocky Mountains walled by rocks hundreds of feet high. But once they finally reached the pass, they found a broad, flat valley twenty miles wide. Although they were now in Oregon Country, they still had another thousand miles to go to their new home.

While they were camped, Little Bear showed Jem how to care for the oxen's torn knees and shattered hooves. They took them down to the banks of a muddy stream and caked their legs in the thick black mud. "The mud can heal," explained Little Bear. Back at camp, Little Bear heated some tar and painted it on the oxen's cracked hooves. It set in solid, sealing the cracks. "In about a week we'll reach one of the toughest parts of the journey. This will help strengthen their hooves," he said.

As Little Bear had warned, the captain told them to prepare for a long trek across a desert. They filled containers with water and cut and collected grass for the animals. At sunrise, the wagons rumbled out onto a dry and featureless landscape. The desert stretched out before them, shimmering beneath a fierce sun.

For the first few days, the wagon train rattled across the hard dusty ground during the heat of the day. The trail was so thick with dust that they couldn't see the wagon in front of them. The dust covered their clothes and their faces in a fine white powder. It filled their nostrils and coated their throats until it made them gag. The burning sun blistered their lips until they had to rub axle grease on them to stop them from splitting. The dry air caused the wooden wagon wheels to shrink and the iron rims that held the wheels together to loosen. Some wheels rolled right off, and families were forced to stay behind to make repairs and to try to catch up with the rest of the group as best as they could.

Under the blazing sun, the oxen lowed with pain and fatigue. Even Goliath fell to his knees in the traces, his tongue lolling and eyes glazed. The water had to be rationed, and Jem felt like a traitor pulling the buckets away from the thirst-crazed oxen. Two of the Murphy's oxen lay down in their yokes and couldn't get up again. They were unyoked and left to die. All along the trail were the staring white skulls and sun-bleached bones of other animals that hadn't made it across the desert.

On the second evening, the captain called the group together and suggested they break camp at 2 A.M. and travel on in the dark. They could rest up during the hot day, and travel on again through the cool of the night. Jem prepared the oxen for the early start. He tarred their shattered hooves and gave them some extra feed and as much water as could be spared. Ma tried to cook the family a decent meal from their meager provisions. They were sick of the stale biscuits and dried salted meat. Ella was getting irritable, and baby Matthew was crotchety too. The last straw for Ella came when she climbed into her dusty bedding. She screamed out, "Ma! Jem! There's something in my bed!" Jem investigated and found a scorpion buried in the sheets.

"I want to go home!" yelled Ella. "This trip was a rotten idea. Why did you have to make us go on, Ma? Why didn't we turn back after Pa died?" Ma didn't reply. For the first time, Jem noticed how pale and exhausted his mother looked.

They were woken in the dark hours by the captain's booming voice calling them out of their beds. Ella and the other children held up lanterns to provide some light as the tents were packed up and the oxen harnessed. The wagon train set out into the black night, the children walking on ahead of the wagons and holding the lanterns high to light a path for the weary oxen.

They traveled like this for the next two nights, resting up as best they could during the hottest part of the day. There wasn't a tree in sight, and no shade for the oxen and other animals. They stood in the fierce sun, their heads hanging and breath coming in short strangled bursts. The hot and dusty travelers slept beneath the wagons in the only shade they could find.

On the fifth day of crossing the desert, Ella reached for the water barrel. "Ma, there's hardly any water left. We're going to run out! What do we do?" Ma looked at her with haunted eyes.

On the seventh day, Jem and Ella found their mother lying unconscious under the wagon. They tried to wake her, but she lay motionless in Jem's arms. Jem tried to think quickly. "Ella, get Swift Arrow. Run!"

U U U

"When did your mother last have water?" Swift Arrow asked.

"I'm not sure," Jem said, holding his mother's bloodless hand.

"I told her two days ago that the water was getting low," said Ella. "She must have stopped drinking to save it for us."

Swift Arrow took the canteen from around his neck, gently lifted their mother's head and dribbled the water into her mouth. At first she lay limply in his arms, then she choked and opened her eyes.

"Swift Arrow, what happened? Where are the children?"

"They're fine. But you need water and rest." He gave her some more water. She pushed the canteen away.

"This is your water. You'll need it."

"The children need your strength." He gave his canteen of water to Jem and walked away.

Before they set out that evening, Jem made up a bed for his mother in the back of the wagon. Although it would be an uncomfortable trip, she was too weak to walk. Ella walked on ahead, carrying Matthew in one arm and the lantern in the other, and Jem spurred the exhausted oxen after her. The oxen had drunk the last of their water, and Jem didn't know how much longer they could go on. He asked the Murphys if they could spare a little water as they had some in reserve since their two oxen died. "Go ask your friends. We ain't got any!" Old Man Murphy snapped at him. Everyone else on the wagon train faced the same problem: very little or no water. They were all hoping for the end of the terrible desert.

In the dark of night, that end finally came. From up ahead came the excited cry, "Water! The oxen have found water!" Goliath tossed his head, and the team quickened their pace. Shortly they joined the others at the edge of a shallow pond.

The next few weeks of the journey took them northwest toward the Snake River. They passed through a weird landscape punctured by craters, springs, and geysers. After the dry desert, it was heaven soaking in the warm waters of the springs and washing off the dust from the trail. Some springs tasted like soda water. One night they camped at Steamboat Springs near a beautiful geyser that made a whistling sound like the steamboats Jem had ridden on the Missouri River.

Their mother was still very weak and the oxen thin and tired when the wagon train rolled into Fort Hall. Like Fort Laramie, Fort Hall was a stockaded trading post. But it belonged to the British-owned Hudson's Bay Company, and the British flag fluttered from the blockhouse. The wagon train would stop here for a few nights to give the travelers time to replenish their supplies, rest the oxen, and fix their battered and broken wagons.

The British captain of the fort welcomed the guests but tried to discourage them from traveling on to Oregon. He told them stories of wagon parties that had become stuck on the difficult and steep trails ahead. Many people had been forced to abandon their wagons. Jem's mother turned to Jem and asked uncertainly, "Jem, do you think we should go on?"

"Yes. We've made it this far. We must go on," Jem said, certain for the first time.

"Then you'll need this to trade for food and supplies," she said, handing Jem her wedding ring.

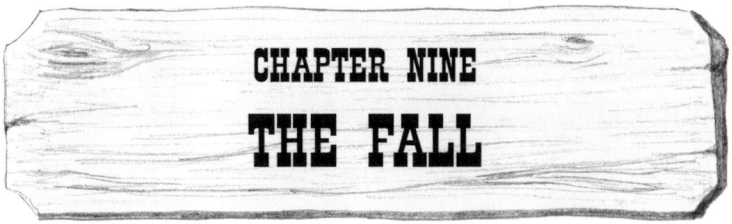

CHAPTER NINE
THE FALL

Jem traded his mother's gold ring for the supplies that they would need for the rest of the journey. He also had the oxen reshod and repairs made to the wagon. The Murphys and some of the other families who had lost oxen were forced to have their wagons chopped down to half their size and refitted with only two wheels. This meant they had to dump even more items, leaving them with only food and water.

After resting for a few days, the wagon party was on its way again, its number greatly reduced from the original sixty wagons that set out more than four months ago. Now only forty wagons rattled along the trail, their boxes battered and canopies gray and torn. For many days, they followed the twisting and turning course of the great Snake River. In some places, the river flowed through narrow canyons, and the oxen were forced to leave its banks and haul the wagons up the surrounding hills. The travelers could see the surging waters below and hear the rumble and roar of many waterfalls.

Jem loved this land and the wild river that flowed through it. In the evenings as they camped near the river, Little Bear showed him how to fish for trout. He made a long-handled shaft out of wood and carved a spear tip from bone. Once it was dark, they went down to the river with a torch to attract the trout. And by the light of the torch, they fished from a jutting ledge of rock.

While they fished, Little Bear told Jem about the legend of Coyote and the creation of the Nez Perce. Once, Coyote fought a terrible monster who had swallowed all the fish and animals on the Earth. Coyote cut out the monster's heart and told the animals to run out though the opening. He then created the

Indian tribes by scattering the monster's body across the land. He made the Nez Perce from the blood on his hands sprinkled with water, saying that they would be few in number but very strong.

Late one afternoon, after the wagon train had been climbing uphill for most of the day, they reached a dead end in the trail. It was as if the path had dropped right off the mountainside.

"We'll have to lower the wagons and oxen down," yelled the captain. They were organized into groups to help lower each wagon and team down the steep slope one at a time. Long ropes and chains were tied to the axles of the wagons, and trees were cut to use as chocks on the wheels.

The Murphys insisted that their team could get down the slope without the help of ropes and men to hold the wagon back. They tied a tree to the back of their wagon to drag on the ground and act as a brake. "The hill gets steeper lower down," warned Swift

Arrow, who had ridden his horse down to check the path. "The tree will not be enough to stop the wagon."

"We don't need your advice," Old Man Murphy snapped, and the Murphys set off over the hill.

One by one, the wagons were lowered down the steep hill. It was a slow and backbreaking process. When it came to Jem's turn, he led the team down while Swift Arrow, the captain, and six other men held onto the ropes. Goliath's position was changed from head of the team to the back. Because he was the strongest, he was the best brake for the wagon.

The chocked wheels slid and the wagon butted up against Goliath. The men fought to hold the wagon at a steady pace by heaving back on the ropes. As the path neared the bottom, it fell away sharply. The wagon rocketed forward, and no matter how hard the men strained on the ropes, the wagon slammed against the haunches of the oxen.

Goliath took the full force, bracing himself against the wagon's weight. Blood trickled down his legs from where the wheels hit.

"Whatever you do, don't let them break into a run or we'll lose it," called the captain.

Jem spoke reassuringly to Goliath in the way he had learned to do. Goliath braced himself against the load, holding the wagon steady. Jem could see Ma and Ella staring nervously up at them from the bottom of the hill. It looked a long way down, but Jem knew they could make it. "Slowly, boy. That's it." Goliath and the other oxen managed to keep their footing in the loose shingle, the wagon slipping and sliding down behind. Gradually the ground leveled out and they safely reached the bottom.

The Murphys hadn't been so lucky.

CHAPTER TEN

INTO THE MOUNTAINS

The Murphys' wagon lay upturned in a ditch at the bottom of the hill, its contents spilled all around. A wagon wheel was splintered and the wagon box twisted and bent out of shape. One ox was stretched out on the ground, and the other hobbled around on three legs. Billie Murphy and Little Bear were kneeling alongside the fallen ox, Billie holding its huge head in his lap. "He's only winded," Little Bear told the downcast Billie, "but the other one will need a few days for the leg to heal. They won't be pulling any wagons for a while."

The rest of the Murphys were trying to right the wagon. They were finding it impossible to move, lying as it was in the bottom of the ditch. Jem unhitched Goliath and his team and led them over. He ran a chain from the axle of the wagon to the yokes of the oxen, and with the oxen pulling and the men pushing, they managed to haul the Murphys' wagon out of the ditch.

The captain rode up and exchanged terse words with Old Man Murphy, "You're a difficult man, Frank Murphy. This wagon train can't wait for you. We reach Fort Boise in two days where we'll rest up. If you can catch up with us there, well and good. If not, good luck to you."

"But one of our oxen is lame!"

"You should've thought of that before driving it down the hill!" replied the captain as he rode off.

Jem felt bad for the Murphys. There was no way they could catch up with a lame ox pulling their wagon. It would take them at least a day to repair the wagon before they could even get on the road. Jem decided to speak to his mother about lending them one of their four oxen. It was only a few more days to the fort, and Goliath was so strong he could make up for the missing ox.

She smiled when he asked. "Yes, Jem, if you think we can still make it to Fort Boise."

The Murphys said very little when Jem handed over the ox. They had already begun work on their broken wagon when the wagon train pulled out. Goliath was now on his own at the head of Jem's team. He led the wagon across rolling hills and into Fort Boise.

The fort was another Hudson's Bay Company stronghold serving the beaver trappers of the region. There weren't many trappers left now that the beaver fur trade was on the decline. The huge populations of beaver that once lived in the rivers of the Rockies had almost been hunted out. The trappers lived alone in the isolated mountains for most of the year, coming down mainly to trade.

The trappers told Jem tales of the road ahead. Beyond the fort lay the Blue Mountains where the trees stood over two hundred feet tall. They said that some of the trails were so steep that you thought you were climbing to heaven. And beyond the Blue Mountains lay the Cascade Range where the mountains were even higher!

Jem knew that the trappers wanted to frighten them. One thing they said worried everyone though: winter was coming early this year. The travelers had already begun to feel the crispness of the dawn and heard the honking of Canada geese as they passed high overhead on their migration south. Early winter snows could close mountain passes and trap the wagon train as it tried to cross the mountains.

On the eve of their departure, a trapper spoke to the group about a shortcut that the wagon train could take and chop days from their journey. "That way you'll be sure to beat the snows," he said. Swift Arrow warned them that the mountains were full of unpleasant surprises. They might promise easy and quick routes, but they only led to dead-end canyons and impassable ridges. People on horseback might be able to get through, but not oxen hauling wagon trains with families.

Jem fell asleep thinking about Swift Arrow's warning. Suddenly he was in a nightmare world of towering mountains and ghostly rivers. In the nightmare, he was clinging desperately to the side of a mountain. Below him was a sheer drop into nothingness. A wheedling voice was telling him, "Go on. It's the quickest way. Go on! Jump! Jump!" But from somewhere else came the urgent grunts and growls of the grizzly bear trying to warn him. The bear was calling him back, back, back to consciousness.

Jem was on the lookout for the Murphys the entire time they were at Fort Boise. He'd almost given up hope when they finally straggled into the fort. They were worn out and pale, though their faces still showed signs of relief that they'd caught up with the rest of the group. They led Jem's ox over, and Old Man Murphy muttered a begrudging thank you. Billie didn't say a word.

Now that the wagon train was on the road again there was a new sense of eagerness in the air. They had only about five hundred miles left to go. Ahead of them might lie the Blue Mountains and the Cascades, but they'd already come over fifteen hundred miles of tough terrain and survived.

At Farewell Bend they said good-bye to their companion, the Snake River. Their trail lay to the northwest and the foothills of the Blue Mountains, while the Snake headed northeast. At windswept Flagstaff Hill, Jem caught his first glimpse of the Blue Mountains. He could see how they got their name. From the distance they shimmered a gray blue in the afternoon sun, their tops iced in snow.

In the Grande Ronde, a beautiful green valley ringed by snowy mountain peaks, the wagon train stopped for the day and they prepared to cross the mountains ahead. Jem took time out from his chores to go riding with Little Bear. Lightning cantered along the valley floor, his head up and ears pricked. But Little Bear hung back on his horse, and Jem wondered if something was the matter.

Jem drew Lightning to a stop and waited for Little Bear to catch up. Little Bear didn't speak as they rode together through the valley. "The horses don't seem to want to race today. Do you think something's the matter?" Jem asked.

"They want to go home. They know it's very close, just over those mountains," Little Bear nodded toward the northeast, "I would like to go home too."

"Won't you be going home at the end of the trip?" Jem asked.

"My father says there is nothing there for us any longer."

"What about your family?"

"The people in the first wagon train my father guided across the mountains got a terrible illness. My father came home sick. Then people in our tribe got sick. My mother was the first to die. Many others followed."

"Do you have any family left?" Jem almost whispered.

"I have some. But my father blames himself for my mother's death. And he thinks it's his fault people in our tribe got sick and died. He cannot face going home."

Little Bear spurred on his horse and galloped back to camp, leaving Lightning and Jem far behind.

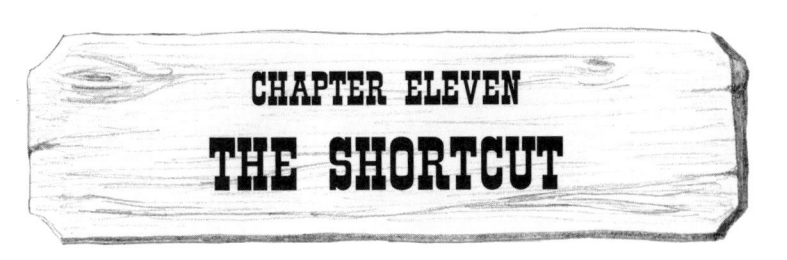

CHAPTER ELEVEN
THE SHORTCUT

For several weeks, the wagon train passed over a land of low-slung mountain peaks and heavily wooded slopes. The air smelled of pine, and soft needles carpeted the trail. The children gathered wild berries and climbed the tall trees. They made slingshots and fired at imaginary bears in the forest.

On a chilly mountain morning, the wagon train came to a fork in the trail. The main path headed up a steep hill; the other followed the meandering path of a river.

"This is the shortcut the trapper told us about," called the captain. "We'll take the shortcut and follow the course of the river." Everyone was pleased they wouldn't be trying to tackle the hill – everyone except for Swift Arrow.

"That is a trappers' trail," said Swift Arrow. "The trappers go into the mountains to hunt and come out again. They do not pass through. There is no way to get through the mountains here."

"I'm taking the shortcut. If others want to follow you, it's up to them." The captain rode on. Everybody geed their oxen on and followed the captain. Jem and his mother hesitated.

"We must follow Swift Arrow and Little Bear. They know the mountains," said Jem.

"But we can't leave the group," Ma said.

"Please, Ma. I had a dream about this. We shouldn't go this way."

"Jem, that was just a dream! We have to go with the others."

For several weeks, the trail followed the path of the river along a green and pleasant valley.

There was plenty of grass for the oxen along the riverbank and shelter under the tall pines for the campers at night. Perhaps the captain and trapper had been right, thought Jem. This was the easiest part of the trip yet.

Very slowly, the valley began to narrow. The rocks crowded in on both sides. They grew taller and steeper until they were leaning menacingly over the path. The travelers found themselves in a narrow cutting in a mountain. It was as if the mountain had been sliced open with a giant knife, and they were struggling along a deep wound. The crack was so narrow and the mountain so high that only a slit of sky could be seen above. It was dark and dank, and the rocks dripped with moisture. The river ran alongside them, no longer a thing of dancing blue beauty but black and sullen. The oxen picked their way along the stony trail, the wagons scraping up against the sides of the wet rocks.

They followed the trail until darkness fell and what little light they had from above was extinguished completely. There was no room to stop and set up camp along that narrow trail. They would have to travel on through the night. Once again, the lanterns had to be lit and the children walked on ahead carrying them high to light the way. They looked like a procession of fireflies crawling through a long dark tunnel.

It wasn't until the light of day that the trail began to open up. The wagon party spilled out onto a narrow plain. Jem gazed up in dismay. The plain was enclosed by the tallest mountains he'd seen. From this distance it didn't seem there was any way out except straight up. They would have to climb now.

The shortcut had taken them into an area that wasn't marked on their maps. The captain was convinced that they would join up with the main trail soon, so the wagon train pushed on westward. They had already lost several weeks following the shortcut, and to turn back now would eat up more valuable time. The wagon train rolled across the plain toward the western mountains and began the uphill climb.

The oxen toiled against their traces and hauled the wagons up the never-ending slopes. At one stage, the trail became so steep that it looked like the oxen would fall backward and onto the wagons. "We need some big chunks of wood to drive beneath the wheels," Jem called out to Ma and Ella as he braced himself against the back of the wagon. Ma handed a piece of wood to Jem, and Jem drove it under the wheels, stopping the backslide of the wagon. Up ahead, Goliath threw himself into the hill and dragged the rest of the team and the wagon up with him. Many of the other teams couldn't make it up on their own. Oxen had to be unhitched and sent back down to help, some wagons being hauled up by eight or more exhausted oxen.

Everyone remained huddled around their campfires long into the evenings. The nights were becoming colder, and the bedrolls were no longer warm enough. Jem thought about the blankets and warm clothes they'd thrown out earlier on to lighten the load. In the mornings, they looked nervously toward the somber gray sky for the first signs of snow.

The snow couldn't have arrived at a worse possible time for Jem. The wagon train was inching its way along a narrow path carved into a mountainside. A vertical cliff was on one side and a sheer drop on the other. There was only enough room for the wagons to pass in single file. The oxen moved on ahead cautiously, hugging the cliff. They probably would have passed by safely if it hadn't been for the snow.

It fell without warning in sudden soft flurries. Soon it was driving in and Jem had difficulty seeing ahead. Ella and Ma, holding Matthew, were walking behind the wagon, trying to keep warm and dry. The snow was building up in piles on the ground, and the path was becoming slippery and slushy as the wagons ahead pushed on.

Jem wasn't sure how it happened. The wagon wheels must have slipped on a chunk of snow and lost traction. The wagon slid up against the two back oxen and they lost their footing. Jem saw Goliath brace himself to steady the team. It was too late. They were all pushed forward in the slippery snow. Goliath and his teammate dropped off the side of the mountain.

"No!!!" screamed Jem, "Goliath!" Jem ran to the side of the mountain to find Goliath and the other ox scrambling against the rocks at the top of the sheer drop. The two oxen behind were trying to regain their footing as the wagon rolled forward, threatening to topple them all off the mountain. Quickly, Jem grabbed some rocks and chocked the wheels. But he knew it wouldn't be enough to hold back the weight of Goliath and the other ox.

"Everything's gonna go!" yelled Old Man Murphy, whose wagon had been traveling behind Jem's. "Cut those two front oxen loose or you'll lose the lot!"

Jem knew he was right. He pulled out his knife and scrambled down to where Goliath was still struggling. His heart sank at the thought of sending Goliath crashing to the rocks below.

As he bent over to cut the traces they suddenly tightened. The back oxen dug their heels in and started to pull away from the precipice. The wagon was being hauled back! Jem could hear the Murphy boys yelling, "Pull, come on ya mangy brutes! Pull!" They'd hitched their own oxen to the back of Jem's wagon and were hauling with all their might. Goliath and the other oxen were able to get a foothold on the rocks and clamber away from the cliff face. Within minutes, the wagon, Goliath, and the rest of the team were standing on firm ground.

Jem thanked the Murphy boys, but Billie just said, "Get yer wagon out of the way, greenhorn!" and gave a mighty grin.

CHAPTER TWELVE

THE ROCK OF THE BEAR

The wagon train continued its climb up mountain slopes now slippery with fresh fallen snow. The travelers desperately searched for a pass through the mountains. But every trail they followed only took them higher and higher.

Jem couldn't fall asleep in the bitter cold. He lay in his bedroll and listened to the troubled breathing of his mother and sister and prayed for sleep and the dreams it might bring. He needed to see the bear. He knew the grizzly was trying to tell him something. When the bear did come, however, it had a message that Jem could not understand.

In the dream, Jem was walking on a long white cloud. It was very beautiful, but with each step, Jem was sure he was going to slip right through. Just when it seemed he would drop to his death, the bear appeared. It wanted Jem to follow it. Jem took an uncertain step toward the grizzly, and the cloud began to harden beneath his feet. He was on safe and solid ground again! Then the bear lay down and rested its great head between its paws. In front of Jem's very eyes, the grizzly turned into a massive black rock. Jem reached out and touched the rock. It was hard and cold. Jem woke with a start.

Later in the day as the wagon train struggled up the mountain, Jem saw a strange black rock off to their right. There was something familiar about its black shape against the white snow. Then he recognized it. It was the rock in his dreams. It was the bear! Finally he understood the bear's message. That was the way they had to go to safety, toward the rock!

Jem leaped onto Tess and rode up to join the captain and Swift Arrow at the head of the wagon train.

"Captain, I think we should go that way," Jem said, pointing to the bear rock, "toward that big black rock between the mountains."

"And what makes you think that? Some built-in compass?" the captain laughed.

"I think there's a pass there."

"Then you've got better eyes than me, boy. Go on, get back to your oxen."

Jem turned to Swift Arrow, "Please listen to me, Swift Arrow. I'm sure there is a way through. The bear told me!"

Swift Arrow looked toward the outcrop of rocks. His eyes narrowed. "The boy could be right, Captain," he said, "there's no snow on the rocks. Wind could be funneling down a pass there and melting the snow." But the captain had already ridden on ahead, his hat pulled forward, his face set.

The weather worsened as the day wore on. The snow was no longer powder-soft against their faces, but stung with the fury of a thousand hornets. Ma and Ella wrapped their shawls around their faces, and Ma cradled Matthew in her arms as they battled up the hill.

The oxen floundered on in the deepening snow until their exhaustion brought the wagon train to a complete stop. They would have to rest until the storm passed. The travelers sought shelter under some scrappy pines. The snow was too thick on the ground to pitch their tents, and they were forced to sleep in their wagons. Ma, Ella, Matthew, and Jem lay side by side in their cramped wagon. Outside, a strong wind beat against the wagon canopy and howled eerily.

"Ma, do you think all those stories about the Donner Party were true?" Ella asked as they listened to the wind. They'd all heard the passing travelers' tales about a wagon train trapped by snow in the mountains the winter before. The stories filtering through said that over half the men, women, and children had either starved or frozen to death. Some said the survivors had been forced to eat their dead companions in order to survive.

"You know people exaggerate, Ella," Ma said, "and the Donner Party were going to California, not Oregon. They'd gotten lost, and we're not lost."

Yes we are, thought Jem. Though he didn't say that. Ma knew they were lost too, only she didn't want to worry Ella.

Jem had known all afternoon what he had to do. He waited until the dead of night when Ma and Ella were fast asleep and the other wagons were quiet. He left his mother a note and sneaked out of the wagon to saddle up Tess. He was worried poor old Tess couldn't make it through the snow. But he had to try.

Unlike the night on the prairie, Jem was prepared this time with lantern, matches, clothing, and food. He was trying to load the pack saddle in the dark when he heard a noise. The guards. Now they'd want to know what he was up to. Jem looked out into the dark and saw a ghostly white shape approaching. It was Lightning! Little Bear was riding him.

Wordlessly, Little Bear leaned forward and pulled Jem up behind him. The two riders slipped quietly into the freezing windy night.

Little Bear waited until they were out of earshot and said, "My father told me what you saw today. I knew you would go back to the rock."

The wind whipped up the mountainside and hurled snow in the boys' faces as they clung to Lightning's back. Jem carried the lantern until the wind snatched it out of his hands. They rode on in the darkness. They couldn't see a thing in front of them; all they knew was that they had to keep heading straight down the mountain to retrace the wagon train's path.

Lightning was brave and surefooted. He stepped out into the blackness, picking his way carefully down the mountainside. Jem felt as if they were walking off the face of the Earth into a freezing black void. The cold wind cut through their flesh and chilled their bones.

They fought their way slowly through the long cold night. Jem and Little Bear took turns riding in front, the back rider getting some shelter from the blasting wind. At some stage, the snow stopped falling, but the wind wouldn't give up its attack. It hurled itself against them like an invisible battering ram, and it was Lightning who was hit with its full force. He didn't flinch, only slowing down if he sensed the boys slipping from his back.

A pale dawn rose to greet the tired riders. Jem peered through the growing light for any sign of the rock. "There it is. There's the bear!" he finally cried, pointing along the mountainside.

"It does look like a bear!" Little Bear called back above the wind. "It's crouching between the mountains with its long snout between its paws. It looks like it's about to leap off the mountain!"

Before setting off toward the rock, Jem tied a bright ribbon from Lightning's saddle blanket to a tree so that they would know their way back to the camp. As they got closer to the huge rock, they could see that the front legs of the bear straddled two slopes. The bear was crouching over a narrow path between the mountains. "You were right, Jem. The bear is guarding a pass!"

The boys followed the pass a little way into the mountains. It showed no signs of ending. Instead, it widened, gently pushing the mountains aside. The snow was not as deep and the going was easy.

"We have to ride back and tell the others, Little Bear. The wagon train can easily get through here."

CHAPTER THIRTEEN

THE WAY HOME

Jem and Little Bear followed the path back along the mountain until they found Lightning's ribbon tied to the tree. Then they began the long uphill climb back to camp. They were so excited with their news that the cold no longer mattered. The wind had dropped, and sunlight pushed its way feebly through the clouds. Lightning's step was light and quick, and it wasn't long before the camp emerged out of the snow.

Jem's mother ran to his side and gave him a hug. "Swift Arrow knew that you would make it back," she cried with relief.

"We found a pass through the mountains, Ma. We have to tell the captain!"

But when Jem found the captain, he didn't want to know. "Go back to your wagon and get ready to pull out, boy. We don't have time to listen to your crazy dreams." He mounted his horse and went to ride off.

"But we saw the pass!" cried Jem, grabbing the reins. "It leads through the mountains!"

"Let go of my horse," the captain bellowed, and then turning to Swift Arrow, he said, "Take this boy back to his mother, Swift Arrow, before I lose my temper."

"We should listen to him, Captain. At least go back and check out his story."

By that time, some of the others in the wagon train had overheard the argument. A group of them gathered around.

"What's this about some pass, Captain?" Old Man Murphy called out.

"The boy has some crazy notion about a way through the mountains back there. It looked like a bunch of rocks to me."

"We've seen it!" Jem insisted.

"It probably goes for half a mile into the mountain and then pulls up short against a cliff face. I say we have to go on," the captain said.

"Yeah, and what does Swift Arrow say?" Old Man Murphy asked.

"We should go back," Swift Arrow replied.

"Then I'm following Swift Arrow," Old Man Murphy announced strongly to those gathered around.

With that, the others turned back to their wagons and prepared to follow the Murphys' lead. The captain looked levelly at Swift Arrow, and without any trace of bitterness said, "Well, Swift Arrow, it looks like the boy has won the day. I don't know what makes you so convinced that he's right, but let's go and find out."

"Thank you for believing in me, Swift Arrow," Jem said when Swift Arrow rode alongside their wagon.

Swift Arrow pulled up his horse and looked down at Jem. "You were brave to make your peace with the bear," Swift Arrow said. "You are worthy of belief."

"Why can't you make your own peace, Swift Arrow? Why can't you go home?" Jem asked Swift Arrow. Swift Arrow didn't reply. He stared ahead of him into the distance as if he hadn't heard a word.

The wagon train traveled for two days along the mountain pass. Sometimes Jem wondered if they would indeed come to a dead end, but he trusted in the bear. His friend had not been back to visit him in his dreams, and Jem knew he would never see the bear again.

On the afternoon of the second day, the captain called out from the head of the wagon train, "Mount Hood. I can see Mount Hood!"

Jem urged Goliath and the team on, and the pass began to widen out ahead of them. As they turned a bend, the snowcapped cone of Mount Hood rose up to greet them.

"Below Mount Hood is Willamette Valley," Swift Arrow explained to Jem, Ma, and Ella. "You are nearly home."

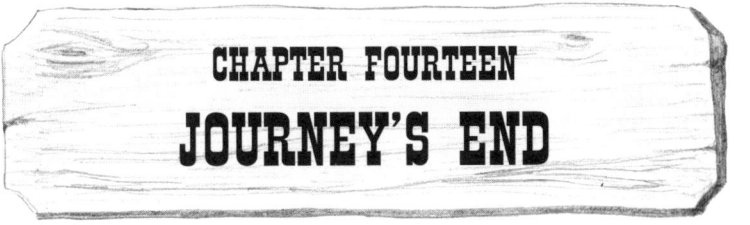

CHAPTER FOURTEEN

JOURNEY'S END

They had only a few more weeks of travel left ahead of them. Everyone was excitedly making plans for when they would arrive in Willamette Valley. Some would go on to Oregon City, but most planned to settle in the fertile valley that they'd all heard so much about.

Jem, Ma, and Ella talked about the land they would own and the first home that they could truly call their own. They playfully argued about what they would farm. Ma wanted to grow apples so she could see them blossom in the springtime, Ella wanted to breed horses, and Jem wanted to farm with the oxen he'd come to love thanks to Goliath. Secretly, he also dreamed of breeding horses as quick and clever as Lightning. He would miss Lightning when the journey was over, but he would miss his new friend Little Bear even more.

Little Bear was very quiet when they talked about their new home. Jem knew it was because he was thinking about his own home and family. He wondered where Swift Arrow and Little Bear would head now that the journey was nearly over. Swift Arrow would probably guide yet another group of emigrants across the long and dangerous trail. It was not much of a life for Little Bear.

Early one morning as Jem was harnessing the oxen, Little Bear came up leading the horses. His father's horse was packed high with gear, and Jem realized that the time had come for good-bye. He felt a sharp pang of sadness.

"I've come to say thank you," Little Bear said to Jem. "My father told me this morning that we are going home. He said that you spoke to him, and it touched his heart. Because of you, I will see my family again."

Little Bear took Lightning's reins and handed them over to Jem. "He belongs with you. You have both been brave and good friends." Before Jem could say anything, Little Bear turned and walked away.

FROM THE AUTHOR

I love reading about great journeys. Part of me would love to saddle up my horse and head out on some great overland trek of my own. But I doubt I would have had the courage to cross the Oregon Trail.

In researching this book, I read lots of diaries written by those who made the journey. They were very brave people. It was a long tough passage across a wild and lonely land – but the things they saw! Imagine the prairie covered in buffalo as far as the eye could see, or a vast desert bathed in a blood red setting sun.

In parts of the United States today, you can still see the deep ruts cut in the ground by the wagon wheels as pioneers crossed the Oregon Trail. Perhaps one day I will just saddle up and follow those tracks, and see where the Spirit takes me.

Susan Brocker

DISCUSSION STARTERS

1. Jem and his family travel a great distance to find a better life for themselves. Have you ever had to travel to a new place? If not, where do you think your family would have more opportunity, and what hardships can you imagine might come with that?

2. When two of the Murphys' oxen die and one becomes lame, Jem lends them one of his family's oxen. Why do you think he made this sacrifice? Have you ever sacrificed something for another person? What was the situation?

3. Discuss the ways this story relates to the saying, "The grass is always greener on the other side." Do you think this saying applies to this story? Why/Why not?